# Lovely Pink

## RAINE MILLER

NEW YORK TIMES BESTSELLING AUTHOR

Copyright © 2021 Raine Miller Romance
All rights reserved.
Cover Design: Letitia Hasser
Cover Image: Sara Eirew
Editing: CC Readings
Proofreading: Proofing with Style

ISBN-13: 9781942095392

Raine Miller Romance

The best way to predict the future is to create it.

-ABRAHAM LINCOLN

# CONTENTS


Epigraph v

Acknowledgments viii

Chapter 1 1

Chapter 2 17

Chapter 3 32

Chapter 4 50

Chapter 5 71

Chapter 6 79

Chapter 7 93

Chapter 8 104

Chapter 9 121

Chapter 10 128

A Note from Raine 137

About the Author 141

Books by Raine Miller 143

SEAL OF THE PRESIDENT OF THE UNITED STATES
E PLURIBUS UNUM

# Acknowledgments

A VERY SPECIAL THANK YOU goes out to Jana Aston for her invitation to write this little book in the first place...originally as part of the *Love in Transit* anthology back in 2017. Along with her and four other lovely ladies, we each had to come up with an idea for our heroine to be riding the subway in a wedding dress after a rough start to her day. Which is why you get Reese on her way to a costume party in Washington DC dressed in full regalia, and then exiting the metro at the **CAPITOL SOUTH** station, which as it happens, was the original title of this story.

# CHAPTER 1

## REESE

*October*
*Washington DC*

A red shirt with the Netflix logo taped in place, and a fake bag of ice.

How very clever.

I wish I could've thought of such a brilliantly simple idea before I decided to put on what I'm wearing right now.

To be clear, that would be *wearing, while riding the DC Metro* to my selected destination for the evening on the busy Saturday of Halloween weekend.

I tried not to pout over how much more I would've enjoyed a nice, safe dose of Netflix & Chill with Horatio curled up in my lap instead of going out tonight, but I promised my friends from work I would come. So, I'm on my way to a Halloween party. Make that a "costume required" Halloween party.

Bleh.

I guess I sort of blend in, considering Mr. Netflix & Chill and I aren't the only ones wearing costumes on the subway tonight.

There's a guy rocking a lavender unicorn suit, complete with sparkly rainbow tail and twisty horn, who just gave me and my dress the sideways-eye. *Heyyyy, like you're in a position to judge me, Fluffy.* His buddy, Suicide

Squad Joker sporting some painfully green hair, leans in and snickers at something Fluffy just whispered in his ear, most likely about me and my dress. *Yeah, and you're no Jared Leto, you ass. Good luck with that green hair in about a week from now.*

Sometimes I hate people.

A drop of sweat rolls down my back as the interior of the train car starts to feel chokingly claustrophobic.

*Slow breath, Reese.*

Like my choice of costume tonight was something that wouldn't attract at least a passing response.

*Riiiiight.*

I'm an idiot. And while I won't argue the validity of that point, I am also a magnet for unwanted attention regardless of whatever I do or don't do. This is reality when your last name is Pinkarver, and you can trace your lineage—in a solid direct line mind you—to a beloved POTUS. My great-great-grandfather served his term nearly a century ago, but the name Pinkarver is still considered political royalty in this town. Right alongside Kennedy and Roosevelt. Others in my family have served in Congress, the Senate, and as governor of two different states of the union. All of this information is written down for posterity, my name in textbooks used in fifth grade Social Studies, all the way up to US History 101 at college campuses everywhere.

Legitimate stuff.

*Unlike me.*

My day started off for shit, and it hasn't gotten any better as the sun made its path across the sky. I'd pretty much written it off for any improvement at this point.

My big toe throbbed behind the heels I was wearing, still protesting the unfortunate smashing of it into the nightstand earlier this morning. The headache I'd battled for most of the day was giving me every indication that it wasn't quite finished with me yet. At least I knew why the headache. A lack of caffeine was the culprit there. Zeke's Brew House got shut down for health code violations (plural) and I'd been running too late to go somewhere else.

So, I guess I'll be finding a new place to get my coffee from now on.

The weird message from my mother last night wasn't helping, either. Something about my inheritance coming due with my twenty-fifth birthday, which was just two months from now. I didn't know anything about an inheritance for when I turned twenty-five. She'd never mentioned it before, so I was a little lost on the topic. My mom currently lives in Japan with her third husband who serves as the US Ambassador to Sapporo, so the time difference usually has us playing phone tag for a bit before we can connect.

Yeah, make that very weird. My whole family situation is weird, though. It's been weird from the very beginning.

My grandfather, Theodore Pinkarver, had already raised three daughters before his only son was born to wife number two. Theodore Junior—my very beloved and "perfect" father. Grandfather had an obsession with his son that did not extend to his daughters, who were already living their own independent lives by the time my dad arrived on the scene. It was just as well, because my grandparents put their efforts into raising their precious son to be the prince who would inherit the Pinkarver kingdom some beautiful day off into a bright and wonderful future.

It didn't work out that way though.

My father's life was nothing even close to my grandparent's vision for him.

He ended up impregnating my mother when he was nineteen and she was just seventeen. My mother wasn't considered quality marriageable material for Theodore Pinkarver's only son, so the two of them were separated by my grandparents, and the scandal buried. My grandfather had the means and the connections to make it all happen with very little fuss.

Then, my very young parents went along with the business of growing up and living out their separate lives. My mom had a baby to raise and husbands (plural) to find. My dad was just getting started on the wild lifestyle he enjoyed so thoroughly.

And so, my grandfather swept the whole business—including me—under the carpet stacked in the closet with the rest of the Pinkarver skeletons. Money was provided to my mother for our support, and nobody knew I even existed.

All neat and tidy.

Until ten years later, when my father managed to kill himself one dark and stormy December night. A freak accident involving an icy tributary of the Potomac, and what was probably far too many drinks before he ever made the bad decision of getting behind the wheel.

His death was definitely the game changer for my grandfather, mostly because it was at this point my existence was finally revealed to the world. Reese Pinkarver, only child of Theodore Pinkarver Jr., sole grandchild of Theodore and Rosalind Pinkarver, was alive and well at St. Mary's School for Girls down in South Carolina.

My grandparents tried to build a framework of bright and happy onto my presence, but it was pretty hard to shiny-up the fact, I had been born illegitimate. The only descendant of the prestigious Pinkarver clan was the "love-child" of two kids who never saw each other again after the pregnancy was confirmed—and kept secret from the world for more than a decade.

Putting a nice spin on that sad story wasn't so easy.

My grandfather couldn't rely on his daughters for replacements because they were past child-bearing age by the time my father died anyway, whether they were married and willing or not. One of my aunts is a dedicated heart surgeon, another a senator of Maryland, and the third is living the bohemian-artist life in Greenwich Village. She's my favorite, in a fun Auntie Mame kind of way. *Life is a banquet and most poor suckers are starving to death!* Yep. "Emotionally starved" is a clever way to sum up the Pinkarver family in a nutshell. What we lacked in births, we made up for in extra "dysfunctional-family."

Recently my own life felt like I was right

on track with the rest of my family with the dysfunction—ergo the reason I am wearing a freaking wedding dress on the subway right now.

I figured I could get away with it for a costume...especially if I slutted up the whole look with makeup, messy hair, and a homemade sign that read RUNAWAY pinned to the skirt.

And yes, I've heard it before—sometimes my good judgment is questionable. My bad judgment? Not so much.

The thing? The dress I'm wearing...is not a costume. Not at all.

It's my real wedding dress.

Well, it *was* my real wedding dress.

It's been hanging in the back of my closet for months, staring at me every time I go in there to choose clothes. Never to be worn. And a designer wedding dress isn't something one can just drop off at the local

Salvation Army without notice either. Undoubtedly someone would find my sad story just sordid enough to leak.

It still surprised me the news of my breakup with Tim had passed with barely a ripple in the press. We'd met at work in one of the reading rooms at the Smithsonian Institute Archives where I helped him locate some zoological records from the Roosevelt Expedition of 1913 to what was then "Amazonia." He kept coming back to SIA asking for me specifically, to *help* him find documentation on some obscure expedition from a century ago.

I couldn't resist the romance of it all.

Yeah, that emotional starvation thing from which all Pinkarver's seem to suffer? It helped me fall hard and fast for the free-spirited archaeologist who'd managed to charm me thoroughly by the end of our first date. I'd snagged my very own Indiana Jones, and I was going to keep him. The fact Tim didn't appear to be all that impressed with my political family tree was an extra bonus.

Nobody was more surprised than me when he popped the question nearly a year later. I said yes. We planned a small but elegant wedding in Charleston where I have extended family on my mom's side. I bought the dress. All was good and we were happy.

Except that it wasn't good, and apparently *he* wasn't happy.

Three weeks before our big day, Tim went on a short work trip to Brazil. He never made his return flight. The morning I was to pick him up at the airport, he sent me an email saying his career was taking him in a new direction and he wasn't ready to get married. He would be staying in Brazil indefinitely, and I was not to come there to be with him.

I had been dumped—and I was crushed.

Tim had completely blindsided me with his explanation for his reasons, the abrupt move to South America, everything.

My grandparents were remarkably supportive of the whole messy business though, assuring me they would make sure the news of our breakup was tamped down in the media. It was in their best interests really—I got it. They didn't want the embarrassment attached to them. It was bad enough they had to acknowledge my illegitimacy at all. If there was a way they could've turned back time and forced my parents to marry, I know they would have done it. Separating my parents was their one true regret. They couldn't even forge documents to show a secret marriage had taken place, because my mom married her first husband when she turned eighteen, right before I was born. At the time, I'm sure my grandparents were relieved to have my mother out of the way and married to someone else who could claim the inconvenient kid.

Who was only a mere girl anyway.

They also assumed my father would have years to live, with plenty of time to give them at least a son or two who could carry on the sacred Pinkarver name. The obsession over babies born with penises in my family is a thing. And in case you didn't already know, Pinkarver penises always trump Pinkarver vaginas. This was the running theme woven throughout all relationships between my grandparents and the rest of us. I also believe that if they could've arranged a sex change for me, they would've done that too. Instead of Reese I could've been Reid. Good thing it's not so easy to grow a penis on a female.

It just wouldn't do, having the news of their illegitimate granddaughter being dumped by her fiancé mere days before the wedding Tweeted, Facebooked, and Instagrammed all over social media. I remember my grandmother repeating the same sentiment at the time, "Thank God, he didn't stand you up at the altar. We could never hold our heads up in this town again."

*Well, lucky for you, Grandmother, you don't live in this town anymore, so you don't have to worry yourself into a dramatic frenzy over it.*

Two years ago they made the Boston house their permanent year-round residence, so I didn't see them much unless I was summoned. Whenever a summons did come, I went to Boston to see what they wanted.

I didn't question the why's or the what-for's anymore. I'd learned my place in the order of things. I was an extension of their political empire, tied by virtue of my bloodline to the one person they had ever truly valued—my father. That's how the purpose of my life worked in their frame of reference. I understood, but it sure would've been nice to be loved just because I was their grandchild and not because of what I represented.

Ahh, but these were merely useless thoughts taking up space in my busy brain.

Just like the notion of having any kind of true freedom to do whatever I wanted in life, was equally useless.

Which is how I ended up with the bright idea to recycle my cursed wedding dress into a Halloween costume and wear it on the metro.

I felt the train slow down as the ticker flashed CAPITOL SOUTH on the digital display in tandem with the recorded announcement.

*Go time, Reese.*

# CHAPTER 2

## REESE

I made my decision in the time it took for me to exit the metro.

This life-altering decision also served the additional purpose of preventing me from stressing over the attention (gaping stares) people were giving as I came out of the tunnel in my *Galina* gown.

I supposed it would be pushing it to grab a coffee from one of the cart stands, but I considered it. My caffeine levels for the day were dangerously low. I reminded myself to take care of that little problem as soon as I got to the party.

But back to my big decision. Tonight, this whole wedding disaster with Tim was out of my life for good. This dress would not be returning to my closet. It was well past the time for me to move on. Tim was gone and he wasn't coming back. I was still alive and kicking, and honestly, no longer emotionally devastated over his departure, either. It was more a feeling of indirection I felt at the moment. Where was I going? What was my final destination supposed to be? Who would be there with me? I had some vague ideas about my future, but it involved another person whose motivations were not completely clear to me just yet. I needed more from him but just wasn't totally sure what *more* meant on my end.

I suppose, wearing my once-beloved

wedding dress to a fun party tonight was a symbolic gesture I was ready to let the past go and move forward.

Relationships, men, weddings—were off the menu as well. Despite one particular person's opinions on the matter, I needed a break from the whole shebang. There were other more important things for me to focus on at the moment.

As I walked the short block down New Jersey Avenue to the address where the party was being held, I got the most unsettled feeling in the pit of my stomach—as if I were standing on the precipice of some great shift about to happen in my life.

That same feeling returned just a few minutes later when I lifted the heavy Victorian knocker on the door to Lance Oakley's house, letting it fall three times in quick succession. Lance is a friend I met when I started working at SIA. He's also the son of our sitting Vice President, so we totally "get" each other. He feels just as trapped by his father's role in government, as I do within the confines of my family. For an Army veteran who lost his left leg below the knee in Afghanistan, Lance is remarkably positive in his outlook on life. If you don't count all those tats he has. He is literally covered from the neck down. I think he gets them as a form of therapy for the PTSD, but tattoos are better than drugs if it's your addiction.

The front door to Lance's house opened before me with a creaking groan, the tired iron hinges in perfect step with the Halloween decorations lining the stone steps and scattered across the landing. I could hear music blaring and people shouting from inside, but I couldn't see who was greeting me.

I tilted my head to peek around the door, but then pulled back quickly, anticipating a horrifying monster face to punch out and scare the crap out of me.

No freaky Halloween gag-greeting exploded from behind the door.

But there *was* something.

Actually, it was *someone.*

And not the host of the party, either.

"Hello, Pink. I've been waiting for you." He smiled, his eyes registering my costume before widening his mouth into an even bigger grin. "That's a very pretty dress, but I think the sign you've pinned to the skirt needs to go, baby. No more running away."

"Gr-aay?" I stuttered, momentarily shocked to see him. Grayson Lash looked as delicious as usual, this time in bespoke gray pinstripe from head to toe. In keeping with the Halloween theme, a nametag in the shape of a crayon with GRAY written on it, in gray magic-marker of course, stuck to his jacket.

"What are you doing here?"

"Lance invited me, but I'm really here just for you, Pink," he answered in his sexy drawl, "and you already know why."

"What do you want, Gray?" I regretted my question the instant the words left my mouth, because he was correct—I did know.

He laughed and shook his head slowly as he stared me down. "You're gonna make me say it again, even though you know exactly what I want." He gave me another thorough perusal, his lingering look in the vicinity of my cleavage making my body heat spike in places that hadn't seen any action in nearly two months. The exact same amount of time since I'd *seen* Gray. "Hell, you're even dressed for it," he added on for clarification.

"Why are you really here?"

"Because I *want* you to marry me," he said clearly.

Gray's tall frame filling Lance's doorway

went a little blurry before my eyes as my vision clouded up. Suddenly, there didn't seem to be enough air left for me to breathe—in all of North America.

I was going down...and it was probably going to hurt.

THERE ARE MOMENTS IN LIFE WHEN TIME moves so fast you can't possibly process what's really happening to you.

This was definitely one of those moments.

"Welcome back." The words fell from soft lips hovering right above mine, the unmistakable sound of relief in his tone. "I wasn't sure if you were breathing there for a minute. I was about to start CPR on you. Don't fuckin' do that again, Pink. You scared the hell out of me." Gray's words were harsh, but delivered gently as his fingers stroked across my temple.

"What happened? What did I—" I tried to sit up from what appeared to be a...bed? "Why am I in Lance's bed?" I asked, confused and disoriented.

He frowned and increased his hold on me. "How do you know this is Lance's bed? Have you been in it before?"

"Yes." My mind was spinning from the unreality of Gray literally on top of me in a bed. I couldn't stop my brain from processing exactly how the weight of him felt pressed against me. *Damn good, unfortunately.*

The warm chocolate brown of his eyes turned dark and his frown deepened. "You have? When? I'ma hafta kill him now."

"Stop it. I've been in his bedroom before, not his bed." I had to admit the possessiveness Gray was displaying didn't offend me. It should have annoyed me greatly, but I found it endearing. It showed he cared about me on some level, the extent to which he cared was still something I was trying to figure out.

"Why in the hell have you been in Oakley's bedroom?"

I pushed against him again in an attempt to get him off. It was like trying to move a brick fence. "This is cute, it really is, Gray, but I don't care for your tone *or* your implications. Lance is a friend and that's all he is. You know this very well, so stop being a stupid ass."

"You still haven't told me why you've been in this bedroom before," he shot back.

"For the record, I don't owe you explanations about *any* of the reasons I go into other people's bedrooms, but if you must know I brought him dinner a few times when he was laid up after his car accident...as any good *friend* would do." Gray's chocolaty eyes blinked down at me, processing the truth of my explanation.

"Oh yeah, his accident," he mumbled a little less possessively.

"Enough with this big, dumb ape routine you've got going." I shoved with both hands to his chest while twisting my lower body as hard as I could, in an attempt to get him to budge. "Will you get off me, Grayson Lash!"

His response was to give me another one of his signature lazy grins before moving off to his side. The second his body separated from mine, I felt the loss of his warm weight almost painfully. I'd also felt an erection when I'd bucked my hips to get him off me.

This was not good.

Gray was the one person who held the power to turn my life upside down, and I could see he was still determined to try. The premonition I'd felt so strongly while walking up the steps to Lance's front door?

That feeling I was teetering on the precipice of a shifting change?

The very one.

Well, Gray had just confirmed precisely what "shift" was going to mean for me—and it meant I was in big, big trouble.

My mind started whirling with facts and details of what I already knew. Conversations that we'd had. Comments made here and there by my grandparents, and even my mother over the years. My mother's strange message about my inheritance coming due made a lot more sense to me now. She misspoke on the phone. It wasn't an inheritance, but rather it was an *inheritance debt* that was coming due with my twenty-fifth birthday.

*Fuck.*

"Why are we up here in Lance's bed anyway? What happened to me?" I managed to ask as my chest started in with the familiar, but unwelcome tightening.

"You went sideways on me in the doorway, so I had to catch you. Lance said to put you in here."

"You carried me up all those stairs?" I asked incredulously.

He cracked a smug grin. "I did." He flexed a bicep into a pose for me. "The extra workouts I've been putting in have really paid off."

"No wonder you had to lie down."

"Nah, I'm kidding. You're a feather, Pink. It was more of a chance to feel you up while I checked your vitals. I mean, I think it's time to *really* get to know each other on a more intimate level before we sign off on this marriage, don't you agree?" Gray loved to tease and flirt with me, and he always had, but this version of him felt very different. He was dead serious.

Instinctively, I started patting my hand

around the bed to locate my purse. I needed a puff off my inhaler before having this conversation with him.

My asthma episodes had a way of showing up at the worst times.

Kind of like Grayson Thaddeus Lash III.

No. I didn't want to believe this was real. He could not possibly be here calling in a promise nobody had ever really taken seriously. *But you know they do.*

Maybe this wasn't asthma at all. I'd hit my head when I went down in the doorway, and my headache was back to maximum pounding, so yeah, it very well could be the effects of a head-injury combined with being trapped inside of a bizarre dream.

The same dream (nightmare) I was most surely having at this very moment.

The one where Gray was telling me we were getting married.

"No, is the wrong answer, sweetheart, and you are definitely not dreaming."

*Dear God, did I just say that out loud?*

"Yes, you did. And *yes*, is the only answer I want to hear out of your pretty mouth. I'll accept a *yes* from you, and then you can give me the date you want for the wedding."

"What wedding?" It came out sounding more like "wha-weh-ing" but Gray totally understood me.

"Our wedding, darling, and don't forget that time is working against us with your birthday only two months away."

*Fuck, fuck, fuck!*

"Oh, we will, Pink, we most definitely will, don't you worry," he said with that sexy Carolina drawl of his that rolled off his tongue, as smoothly as his promise of some hot and dirty sex.

Would the sex be hot and dirty with

Gray?

I already knew the answer to that pointless question, aaaand now I was officially out of oxygen.

"Purse—inhaler," I gasped, before I was unable to do even that.

# CHAPTER 3

## REESE

“I would really appreciate it if you could be done with this whole no-breathing thing. I don't like it.” I held her inhaler up to her mouth. “Big breath in for me, baby,” I coached before propping her to a sitting position against the headboard. “Slow and easy now...let the medicine go to work.”

Her green-gold eyes held mine for just a moment, before she rested her head down on her knees in exhaustion. "Graaay—"

"Shush now. Don't try to talk. You've officially scared the ever lovin' shit out of me, Pink. Breathe...steady and slow. Do you need another hit? Just nod if you do."

She nodded and lifted her head for the inhaler, proving she was able to comprehend my panicked babbling. My hand visibly shaking as I helped her take another puff was my wake-up call that my feelings for Reese ran so much deeper than I'd ever let myself believe.

Jesus Christ, this was terrifying.

I also felt like the biggest shitheel on the planet for being the cause of the goddamn asthma attack in the first place. I fucked up with her tonight and there was no denying it.

"The paramedics are on their way, baby. You're doin' great."

"No—please—I don't want to—" she

protested.

"Yes, you are going to the ER," I interrupted, speaking as calmly as I could manage. "You need to be checked out by a doctor." I left off the part about never sleeping again, if she didn't get examined by a medical doctor at a fucking hospital *tonight*. It was a miracle I didn't need to change my shorts right now. When she started wheezing and sucking in a whole lot of nothing? My heart—just, stopped.

A few tears rolled down her splotchy cheeks, flushed red from the rush of oxygen she was finally taking in as the rescue inhaler did its job. Thank holy fuck. "I'll be with you every second," I said while rubbing circles over her back with my palm.

She leaned her forehead against my chest, and I felt her relax as her breathing steadied, the panic in both of us easing away. The best damn feeling in the world.

I would hold her like this forever if I had to. I couldn't stop touching her now that I'd started. She was mine to take care of. She'd always been mine. This was the woman I was going to marry and make babies with—even if she didn't believe it quite yet.

She would.

I'd been waiting for months to make my move. I'd almost lost her once before to that idiot archaeology professor, and I wouldn't be letting that shit happen again. After he left her, I'd given her some time to get over him. Even if I'd wanted to go slower with Reese, time was a luxury I just didn't have anymore. Neither of us did. The sand in our hourglass was just about gone for fulfilling the terms of her grandfather's will. Only the two of us could make those very beneficial terms a reality by first, getting married before she turned twenty-five, and then second, by having a son whose surname would legally change to Pinkarver-Lash in order to carry on the Pinkarver name in the bloodlines.

And two months was all the time I had left to get her to the altar, and my ring on her finger.

I MET REESE PINKARVER WHEN SHE WAS TEN years old, at a party held in the rose garden at Mount Laurel. My family's historic plantation just outside of Charleston was the perfect setting for our introduction, because the significance of the place helped drive home the importance of precisely what was expected of me. Mount Laurel is the birthplace of Grayson Thaddeus Lash I, former President of the United States of America, and my esteemed grandfather.

I was an eighteen-year-old college freshman—so technically an adult while definitely still very much a kid in the head—

when my father, Grayson Thaddeus Lash II, pointed her out to me in the rose garden, and told me the wide-eyed little girl with the blond curls holding onto her mother's hand in a death-grip, was the person I would marry.

It wasn't even a suggestion by any means, but a requirement. She had been chosen specifically for me, he said. It only made sense that the direct descendants of presidential bloodlines running as blue as ours, were strengthened by making more little Pinkarver-Lash's to add to the ever-expanding family tree.

To be fair, I believe my father was feeling the nostalgic urge to ensure our family's history was carried on because my grandfather had passed just the year before. Something I didn't appreciate until I was faced with the same scenario many years later.

At the time, I let my father's—*You'll marry that girl someday, Gray*—nonsense go through one of my eighteen-year-old ears and right on out the other. I did not care what he or anyone else required of me. I was young, dumb, and full-of-cum, just like every other male in their first year of college. I was all up my own ass perfecting my *skills* with women who were *my own goddamn age* for one thing. Being matched up with a child was downright disturbing. Having my life laid out for me without my input or consent was fucking infuriating. Marrying any person was a foreign concept I couldn't even entertain. Having children?

I was not hearing any part of what he had to say.

Dad could go after one of my sisters in forging his political dynasty with some other sap-bastard, Son-of-America. My own parents had shown me just how painful marriage could be during the course of my whole life. There was no shining example of a loving relationship for me to draw an experience from, so his words meant very little to me.

As the years passed, Reese and I met at more garden parties, charity balls, and even an event or two at the White House. We forged a friendship over time, as I made more of an effort to get to know her while she grew up before my eyes. I found her delightful, and she seemed to look up to me almost like the big brother she never had. The two of us were connected family acquaintances with an easy friendship, and nothing more than that. There were no awkward moments, nothing weird between us whenever we did happen to run into each other somewhere in Charleston or the DC area. The edict my father had given me so long ago in the rose garden at Mount Laurel was pretty much forgotten in the past where it stayed buried.

Until two years ago when Reese and her

family showed up to my father's funeral.

No longer a shy little girl clinging to her mother for security, but a confident beauty who'd grown into a lovely young woman. My whole opinion of her, and how she might fit into my life, changed dramatically with the event of my father's death.

I found a great deal had changed for Reese, and for me, in the thirteen years since the garden party down at Mount Laurel when my dad told me she would be my wife and the mother of my children someday.

That's about the time "it got weird" between us—and I can honestly say the blame was one hundred percent on me. It wasn't Reese's fault I'd been raised with certain expectations from birth. A law degree from Harvard was one of those expectations. A career in the family business of politics was another. I'd accomplished the Harvard Law degree and was working my way up the political food chain with my new term as

Attorney General for South Carolina solidly in place. It was also assumed that my crowning political achievement would be the governor's mansion someday, and it very well could be if all the pieces fell into place as they were supposed to.

The most important piece of that puzzle was in the back of an ambulance being administered a breathing-treatment for an asthma attack, brought on by me being the demanding asshole I was pretty much most of the time.

I'd have to work on that with her, because Reese certainly didn't deserve an asshole for a husband.

And I *would* be her husband. That wedding shit I'd said no to before? It was happening.

My lovely Pink deserved the best husband in the world. She deserved the best of everything life had to offer. Hell, she deserved to be First Lady of South Carolina, and maybe even more, someday.

And she was getting me in the process, even if she wasn't sure she wanted me yet.

She might not be sure, but I was certain she felt the attraction between us. It was definitely there that night two months ago when I came to see her...and we ended up in my suite at The Jefferson for the night.

Reese felt something for me, or she wouldn't have reacted so strongly when I showed up tonight. She wouldn't be gripping my hand so tightly right now or let me hold her while waiting for the ambulance to show up at Oakley's house.

"How are we doing, baby?" I leaned down to ask against her ear so she could hear me.

Her eyes flickered open, and she nodded up at me before mouthing three words I understood as clearly as if she'd been able to shout them. "Stay with me."

"I'll be right here the whole time. I won't leave you," I assured her with a confident wink solely for her benefit, even though I didn't feel so confident on the inside.

My emotions were all over the place, and for good reason. I'd waited far too long to make my move with Reese. By the time I was ready to settle down, she'd already found her professor with the PhD in Pre-Colonial Amazonia or some ridiculous shit, and to my horror, agreed to marry *him*.

I'd blown my chance with Reese, and then it was too late. Someone else had won her heart by being there with her. While I was down in South Carolina finding my footing as head of the family after my father's death, someone else was stealing my woman away.

I learned an important lesson about priorities. I also learned never to assume the outcome of a relationship with another person. My feelings for Reese became crystal clear the moment I realized someone else was taking her to bed every night. She didn't belong in any other bed but mine. It sucked to realize I'd lost her, but I did accept that I was fully to blame.

I'd pushed her away once before and regretted it ever since. She had tried to offer comfort to me when my father died, and I didn't handle myself well at the time. If I'd done things differently with her, we'd surely be married by now with a child or two, or at least working on it. But nope. I was just too fucked up in my own head to see that I was denying myself the one person who was exactly what I needed.

So, Reese found someone else, and she moved on. I tried to move on as well, but I found I sucked at that too.

I buried myself in work and forged ahead with my campaign for Attorney General of South Carolina, which I easily won. The night the election results came in and we started celebrating, I'd learned what a hollow victory it was without Reese by my side sharing it with me.

And then four months ago a miracle happened.

Dr. Doolittle went to Brazil and decided to stay there without her. Money won out over love in his case. I had a strong suspicion that Reese's grandfather paid the professor to break off their engagement. I never knew any details about a deal and went the extra step of telling Theodore Pinkarver up front, *that I didn't ever want to know.* I kept myself at a distance until that fool professor was out of the picture. My involvement never extended any further than praying for some powerful juju to make Dr. Doolittle decide to take the fucking money and leave.

Tonight wasn't the first time I'd asked Reese to marry me. I'd posed the question to her once before, but my timing was bad because she'd just had her heart broken. I'd also been an ass by presenting it as more of a business plan hatched by our families, than something I really wanted. And then we ended up having a night of mind-blowing sex after a lot of wine and...yeah—

This was where the confusion came into the picture for me. I knew I wanted Reese, but I wasn't sure *why* I wanted Reese. Did I love her, or did I love the idea of merging our families into a magnificent political dynasty? I needed to get my shit together and figure that out so I could explain it to her. She deserved the truth most of all, and I wouldn't lie to her by telling her I'd been in love with her for years. It hadn't been like that for me. My feelings for Reese had surfaced with more of a slow burn than anything else. The one thing I was certain about was how much I wanted to make a life with her. There was no one else for me.

She'd had some time to think about it, but not nearly enough. We were just getting started figuring everything out so maybe it was best to have a meeting with her grandfather to clarify exactly what was at stake here.

It was only fair that she hear from him, what had been decided for the two of us a long time ago.

Our families wanted us together, and I wanted her, so...

The ambulance coming to an abrupt halt brought me out of my little trip down Memory Lane and back to the present—the emergency bay of GWU. The rear doors opened to the outside, and I was relieved to see there was a gurney waiting to take her right in. The EMTs did the transfer efficiently, reporting her medical stats for triage to evaluate where she should go next as I followed closely behind.

"Her name?" the intake nurse, Barb according to her ID badge, asked me as we rolled down the hallway toward what I hoped would be a private room.

"Reese Pinkarver."

"Age?"

"Twenty-four. She'll be twenty-five in two months."

"And you are?"

"Grayson Lash," I answered, bracing myself for the question that would come next.

Right on cue, Barb shot inquisitive eyes up from her clipboard. "Like the president?"

I nodded once and left it alone.

"Your relationship to the patient?"

Ahhh, a question I was more than happy to answer for Nurse Barb. I'd given the same reply to the EMTs when I'd demanded to ride along with Reese inside the ambulance.

"My fiancée."

# Chapter 4

## Reese

*iancée?*

Gray and I needed to have a little talk about his false assumptions. Make that a big talk, rather than a little one. Too bad it would have to wait until I could actually talk *and* breathe at the same time. God. I'd been so stupid in not recognizing the signs of an impending asthma attack. I'd been given plenty of clues, like the headache from a lack of caff—

"You'll need to change out of your—um...wedding dress—and put this on before getting into the bed." The nurse who'd been interviewing Gray handed him a hospital johnny and added on, "Your fiancé can help you. Just let me close you guys in behind the curtain for some privacy—"

As I desperately tried to choke out a protest, she yanked the curtain shut and stepped out, but not before loudly announcing, "All the way down to your panties please."

"I'll make sure she follows your directions to the letter, Barb," Gray called back to her through the curtain, while I shot poison daggers at the back of his head with my mind.

"I bet you will, Mr. Lash," Barb replied on a giggle as the sound of her steps faded away.

He swung his head around toward me, and of course, that smug grin of his was right in place like always, but I could see there was also worry behind his gorgeous brown eyes. Gray was faking with the nurse just now about wanting to undress me. I hardly believed it, but I could see he was really worried about me.

I removed the oxygen cannula and set it on the bedside table.

"You need to keep that on, Reese," he said tightly.

"I'll put it back as soon as I'm changed into the hospital gown. I am breathing fine now."

After about a minute of staring at each other, it was clear I was going to have to start the strip show because he wasn't moving. Strangely empowered, I sat down in the chair reserved for visitors and began to undo the straps on my heels. I took my time lifting my skirt up higher than it needed to be for removing shoes, but this was my show. Gray could watch or go home. I wanted to find out if he was affected by me, the woman, at all. I peeked up at him as my fingers worked the tiny buckle open and was surprised again by his rigidly held stance, as if struggling to hold himself back from pouncing on me. He was fighting *something*; I just wasn't one hundred percent sure if that something was an attraction to me.

"Are you going to help me or not?" I asked softly.

He dropped down to his knees instantly, as if my giving permission had flipped a kind of go-switch inside him. He took over with the other shoe, removed it, and then set the pair of oyster satin Manolos neatly under the bed. There was no pause from him before he slid both hands up one leg to the top of my thigh where my stockings ended. I felt his fingers searching for any clasps that might be hiding before he tugged it down. *How very considerate.* "You can just pull them off," I murmured.

He buried his fingers underneath the elastic edge and yanked the sheer stocking down in a furious rush. Then he moved over to the other leg, his touch a bit more confident. But this time, before he searched for the stocking, he pushed my skirt all the way up to the top of my thighs so he could see what he was taking off me. A little more wandering of the fingers along the top edge of the stocking than with the first one, but I could tell he was frustrated by the situation. He wouldn't look me in the eye either.

Gray got to his feet and then pulled me up to standing with him. He put his hands on my shoulders and abruptly turned me so that my back was to him. All of this was done without a word. I could feel his hot stare burning my back as he studied how the dress worked so he could get it off me without damaging it. If he was as careful with the dress as he had been with the stockings, then he would do fine.

"There's a hidden zip in the left side," I offered.

He found the tag to the zipper and took it down slowly, the sound harsh against the soft swish of silk and lace. The bodice fell away from my breasts, and since there was no separate bra underneath, I was bare the second the dress started responding to gravity. I put an arm across myself to cover my nipples, which were tight and aching thanks to Gray's busy fingers on my body. But my nipples were the extent of what I could conceal with only my arm. My breasts are just not that small.

And I really didn't know how much more of this little tête-à-tête I could endure. I was on fire just from the body heat of Gray so near to me. Probably because *I was naked*—apart from panties thanks to Nurse Barb's orders— and *Gray had been the one to get me naked*, having something to do with the sexual tension between us right now. Thank goodness my panties were nothing too racy. Just a simple lace Agent Provocateur bikini in blushing pink. *Awww, how appropriate for the "bride."*

He held my dress open at the floor so I could step out of it. Once my feet were completely free from the skirt, he rose up and came around to my front with the hospital johnny in his hands. I was going to have to take my arm away in order to put the damn thing on, and Gray would see me floatin' freestyle when I did.

"Don't look at my boobs, okay?"

"Don't be ridiculous, of course I'm gonna look," he snapped at me. "Tellin' a man not to look at naked tits all up in his face is on par with tellin' him not to drop the match that's burnin' his fingers, so don't expect me not to look! It cannot be helped, okay?"

Gray's slight Southern drawl became

much more pronounced in his speech when he was agitated or upset. Well, he was definitely agitated and upset, but also so funny, I had to bite down on my bottom lip to keep from laughing at his thoroughly adorable explanation of why a man averting his eyes to naked breasts was not only highly improbable but also outrageously unrealistic.

He wasn't quite done explaining it to me, apparently.

"I'm standin' here in front of my really fuckin' sexy fiancée—who I've just undressed by the way—and you're tellin' me I'm not supposed to look!" Biting sarcasm rolled off his tongue. It would appear that Gray's self-control had come to a complete and abrupt end as he gave the hospital johnny an angry little snap in front of me. "I am not made of stone."

"And I am not your fiancée," I reminded him, secretly happy about the "really fuckin' sexy" part.

"Well, the hospital staff thinks you are, so hurry up!" He jerked the johnny in my direction once more and jiggled it at me.

"Fine." I dropped my arm from across my chest and freed the girls. *I repeat, the girls have been freed and are on public display! Have a gander if you will!*

A soft groan came out of him in the seconds it took to put my arms through the sleeves, so I knew he'd looked just as he'd assured me he would. The weird thing was I didn't care about Gray seeing me naked. It wasn't even the first time. Honestly, I was relieved we were finally doing this sexual dance around each other out in the open, rather than while under the influence. Things had been brewing between us for a good while now. We'd already crossed the sex line anyway, even though I don't remember much from our night nearly two months ago. I'm not even sure how much Gray remembers because we were both drunk when it happened. He was still sleeping it off when my walk-of-shame out of his suite at The Jefferson was happening.

Not our shining moment, but if anything, I did trust Gray to have my best interests in mind. We were connected through family and an elite inner-circle that basically required we protect one another. An encounter was bound to happen at some point, especially since we were both single now. The part where he kept talking about getting married was a bit more confusing. On both of the occasions when Gray had asked me to marry him, our night had ended badly, accompanied with so much drama and trouble I didn't know what to think anymore. I needed some truthful answers for Gray's motivation before I made any kind of decision on the matter. Money was involved from my grandparents on some level I was certain, but I wanted to hear it from him first.

I stood still, allowing him to tie my gown closed as I made some careful observations. Gray's outward reaction toward me was not at all what I'd expected, especially based on the earlier boasts about giving me some more hot and dirty sex, whenever I said yes to marrying him. Gray wanted me. I knew he was aroused right now, because I could smell it on him.

It was desire I detected in the spicy scent radiating from him in waves.

And that monster snake he had going on in his pants was seriously impressive. I regretted that my naked party with Gray was a lost dream of which I had absolutely no memory. There were some flashes of what we had done, but I do not remember specifics about his body (penis) sans clothing. It was rather cruel to know I'd had him inside me, but no mental picture of what he looked like when he was there. Torturing myself with the conceptual images of us together was not helpful in any way whatsoever.

"Why are you mad at me?" I asked after he'd helped me to get settled in the bed, and my oxygen cannula back in place.

"I'm not mad at you."

"Well, you sure aren't acting very happy after you got to see me naked—so what's the problem?" I knew I was pushing him. but I figured I was entitled to some information.

"My lovely Pink, seein' you naked is not my problem, I assure you. My cock is workin' just fine where you're concerned, beautiful." He cupped himself over his slacks and thrust his hips up from the chair. "How do you think I got this, hmm?"

"I hoped it was because you had to undress me," I answered truthfully, although I did find it strange to be so undisturbed by the topic of our open conversation—Gray's hard-on from taking my dress off of me. Could this night get any weirder?

Probably yes, so I shouldn't even ask.

His brown eyes pierced right into me before he spoke. "You're a goddess. There are no other words to describe you better than that. Reese, I definitely want more naked time with you—so much more—but not if I'm gonna send you to the goddamn hospital unable to breathe!" He pulled at his hair with both hands for like the hundredth time tonight. "Fuck!" he barked.

"But you didn't cause this, Gray."

That big lanky body of his, so tightly posed in the chair beside my hospital bed, looked ready to snap in two; his sandy brown hair a tousled mess from so much nervous hand-dragging through it; the frown lines on his handsome face growing frownier by the second.

"I upset you to the point of sending you here in fuckin' distress with a full-blown asthma attack! Baby, how is that not my motherfuckin' fault?"

"Language, Mr. State Attorney General," I scolded gently, sensing he was really beating himself up over this. "Stress can make the symptoms worse, but it won't be the cause for an asthma attack. I wish you would listen to me."

"I'm sorry, baby, so goddamn sorry for doing this to you. I was way out of line tonight and I really hope you'll forgive me at some point—"

"I forgive you." I shut down his rambling repentance with those three little words.

"You do?" His eyes widened in surprise.

I nodded. "Yes." I held out my hand and waited for him to take it. He hesitated for a moment before accepting my gesture, but he did it in the sweetest way. He lifted my hand to his lips and kept them pressed to the back of my hand. "Gray, it's a medical fact that an asthma attack is not brought on by stress. Other factors cause the airways to constrict, but stress is not one of those factors."

"Your fiancée is right. You should listen to her," said the guy in a white lab coat who strode confidently into my room to stop at my bedside. "Dr. Romero, Chief Consult, Emergency Medicine." The good doctor extended his hand first to Gray, and then to me. "I heard we have some VIPs visiting us tonight. How can I help?"

"SO, WHAT I'D LIKE TO DO IS GET YOU IN TO SEE A pulmonologist in the next month or so," Dr. Romero suggested. "How long has it been since you've been to one?"

"Not since high school, probably. My regular doctor writes the prescriptions for my rescue inhalers right now."

"From what you've told me, the caffeine has done the job of self-medicating to control your asthma, but since you experienced a concerning episode tonight, I'd prefer to prescribe a daily medication that works pretty much like the caffeine in your coffee, but with regular consistency."

"I knew that about the caffeine already, and I missed my usual shot this morning, because my corner coffee shop got shut down for a health code violation."

"Seriously, Reese?" Gray scolded.

"How was I supposed to know? It's not like Zeke's is going to share with the public how they regularly violate the health code, Gray," I mimicked back irritably.

"That's not what I meant. I was referring to the fact that you knew about the caffeine and then missed taking any. That can't happen again."

"So, the new meds should solve that issue for you in the future," Dr. Romero cut in, "and it's likely that your rescue inhaler prescription may need an adjustment as well. Your pulmonologist can help you with that."

"But my episodes have always been pretty intermittent. I wouldn't classify my asthma at anything beyond mild." I wanted Gray to hear it, because he seemed overly worried about me when I knew it wasn't necessary.

"And you will likely continue to present with mild asthma in the same way," Dr. Romero assured me, "but it's important to remember as you age, you'll experience changes in your symptoms that may require a new treatment plan to keep you status quo."

"Got it," I said. "I'll find a pulmonologist then." Gray squeezed my hand in support— the same hand he'd been holding since before Dr. Romero showed up.

"A pulmonology consult is also a good idea if you plan on starting a family. You'll want to be seen by a specialist, preferably before you get pregnant, so you know all of the risks—"

"What are the risks?" Gray blurted, interrupting Dr. Romero.

I stared at Gray in surprise, waiting to hear why he was in need of such information.

Dr. Romero hedged the question neatly. "It would be best for the two of you to see the pulmonologist together whenever you decide to start a family. He or she can explain the best treatment options for Reese, to ensure a healthy pregnancy as well as manage her asthma symptoms efficiently."

"So, it's possible for Reese to have a safe pregnancy, even with her asthma?"

"Yes, of course," Dr. Romero assured him with a smile. "I look forward to reading about your healthy babies in the news when they arrive. Those kids will be the closest thing to American royalty as we can get. You know, I hadn't heard about your engagement, but congratulations to the both of you." Dr. Romero took out his phone and held it up.

"Can I get a picture with you guys for my wife? She won't believe this. My charge nurse said you came in wearing your wedding dress. Please don't tell me you've just gotten married and you're spending your wedding night in the ER."

"Ha-ha—no—um, that was just a Halloween party costume I was wearing." I gave Dr. Romero my best-actress performance and a smile, while digging my fingernails into the palm of Gray's hand. Hopefully, hard enough to draw blood.

He quickly extricated his palm away from my abusive fingernails and extended his hand to Dr. Romero. "Thank you, doctor, for all of your help tonight. I very much appreciate you straightening out my beloved, and getting her back to healthy breathing," Gray said, while curling a possessive arm around me. "I won't lie. I was terrified earlier, before you came in here to speak with us."

Another skill Gray had perfected, was

how to pile on the Southern charm until the person on the receiving end was practically drowning in it. Not that they minded even a little bit.

"Doctor, if you would give me your card, I would love to pass along an invitation to our wedding, for you and your wife—if your schedule permits, of course—that is, when the date is announced to the press."

Super. Ultra. Gag. Vomit.

My lying "fiancé" had now dug himself into a trench comparable in size to the Gulf of Mexico. How on earth Gray was going to explain his way out of the mess he'd made tonight was a mystery, but I was sure eager to begin the *discussion* we were having the moment we had some privacy.

"Thank you very much. My wife and I would love that," Dr. Romero said enthusiastically while handing over his card to Gray.

"When can I go home?" I asked.

"You can go now, actually. As soon as you're dressed, we can check you out."

"Fabulous." *One more time with the damn dress.*

Oh...yeah. That dress had a very hot date with the incinerator in my building as soon as it could be arranged.

# CHAPTER 5

## GRAY

L eaving the hospital was a lot more difficult than it should have been. Thanks to the technological world of cell phones and social media, and unfortunately for our privacy, word spreads fast when someone with a name like mine ends up in a public place such as a hospital. I'd been dealing with my name for thirty-three years so I was used to the attention in a resigned sort of way. Grayson Lash could have been substituted for Ronald Reagan or Woodrow Wilson and received the same notice from people. I had a president's name and a president's blood running through my veins.

As did Reese.

Nothing was going to change that fact for either of us.

It didn't help that people got pictures, and most likely video, as we stepped out of the ER and into the waiting Uber, looking like a bride and groom leaving the church. I had to admit, Reese in the wedding gown, and me in my gray *Brioni* were going to appear legit in the pictures that would be posted on Instagram, Facebook, Twitter and every other celebrity news outlet that feasted on such things.

Reese was quiet beside me in the back seat of the Uber car, looking like a princess in her white lacy dress I'd had the pleasure of taking off her tonight. But when she had to put the dress back on again to leave the hospital, she asked me to step out behind the curtain because she did not need my help. Or didn't want it.

I knew she was furious with me.

We needed to talk so badly, but we couldn't yet. At least during the time it took for the driver to navigate the Saturday night traffic to Reese's place in Georgetown, we would have to keep a lid on it. Both of us were hyper-aware of our situation—that we were still out in public for all to judge. I'd already started working on damage control by tapping out an official statement on my phone to be posted in the morning from my office in Columbia:

South Carolina Attorney General, Grayson Lash III, attended a Halloween party at the Washington, DC home of a close friend last night. During the event, he was called upon to aid party guest, Reese Pinkarver, who required immediate medical treatment for an asthma-related condition. Ms. Pinkarver was accompanied by Mr. Lash via ambulance to George Washington University Hospital Emergency Services where she was treated and later released.

I passed her my phone so she could read it, watching for her reaction to what I'd decided to share with the public about us. The decision to include Reese's name, as well as the reason for her medical treatment, was a calculated one. If her name had been withheld, the press would ID her photo within hours anyway, and the speculation behind the reason for secrecy would only be intensified. If her medical condition wasn't disclosed, the suspicion of illegal drug use would come next. I even debated including that we were both in costume for the party, but decided that part could be revealed later if more of an explanation became necessary.

It was at times like this that holding a public office was annoyingly invasive. The media was going to run this story regardless, because it was too tantalizing to pass up. I felt it was better to give them some truthful details, than nothing at all. The press might be marginally kinder in their reporting, but you could never predict how a story like this one would play out no matter what your official statement was.

"That sounds good to me," she said when she was finished reading. I could hear the exhaustion in her voice.

"Tired, baby?"

"So tired, Gray."

"Rest your head on my shoulder and close your eyes if you want," I offered, not sure if she would take me up on it.

She did though.

And it felt fucking wonderful having her leaning on me, the flowery scent of her perfume floating up to me so I could breathe her in with each and every inhale.

Fucking. Wonderful.

REESE SLEPT UNTIL THE DRIVER DROPPED US IN front of the historic row house she'd called home ever since her move to Georgetown. I'd been to her place to pick her up just one other time, on the occasion of my first proposal of marriage.

The first time I asked was too soon after her breakup. She wasn't ready to move on *then*, but I did not sense Dr. Doolittle was an issue for her any longer. Thank you, sweet baby Jesus. This was very welcome news for me. I would take any positive sign from Reese and use it to help my cause.

What was my cause, exactly?

To be married before we celebrated her twenty-fifth birthday as husband and wife.

Sometimes when I had business in DC, we would meet for dinner to catch up with each other. The only time we didn't, was when she was with he-who-must-not-be-named. I also learned how much I missed having Reese in my life during that time. It was an evolution more than any one thing. A slow evolution of my Neanderthal brain once it clued to the fact she'd be beneath the furs of another man in the cave.

Our night together nearly two months

ago, had also been an epic clusterfuck—with not quite the seriousness of tonight's ER visit—but a clusterfuck just the same.

It had also been the best night of my life.

# CHAPTER 6

## GRAY

*Two months ago...*

"**A**re you ever going to marry me, Pink?"

She looked so beautiful sitting across from me poured into a sexy black dress. A little black dress bent on filling my head with the filthy thoughts of what I'd do after taking it off her.

*Please say yes.*

But I knew she wouldn't. Her hand shook a tiny bit as she brought the wineglass to her lovely lips and finished what was in it. The only small tell visible enough for me to know she was still hurting. Reese could play the Steel Magnolia role very well, which ironically, was part of the reason why she was so perfect for me. Reese Pinkarver was a very strong woman.

"Ask me that question a year from now, please," she said with a pointed look at the bottle of Riesling sitting innocently on our table at Plume inside The Jefferson, my preferred hotel whenever I was in the city. I took the hint and refilled her glass before she had to ask me.

"There is no way I'm waiting a damn year. A month works better for me." I knew my teasing wouldn't bother her, because she was used to me. I'd always talked to her this way. Flirting and dirty talk were my specialty.

"You can't tell me you've ever taken any of that marriage talk about us seriously, Gray."

"Of course, I take it seriously. We have far too much in common for us not to get married and have some Pinkarver-Lash babies the whole world will fall into a full-blown swoon over. You know I'm right, Pink." The image of the two of us *making* one of those babies had me needing a discreet adjustment of my cock below the table. I could just picture her all spread out in the bed with nothing but skin between us. I could worship that body of hers—and I would—if she'd ever let me.

The look she gave me over her glass was a mixture of sadness and caution, her green and gold eyes flickering down after a moment to escape my scrutiny. I didn't need any explanation of the reasons behind her feelings. The sadness was understandable, of course it was. Her fiancé—whom she'd loved even if the cocksucker hadn't deserved it—had left her with little explanation, and he had done it very cruelly.

I knew where Reese's cautionary feelings came from as well. Those were a result of my bad. The one time she let me know she wanted to be with me, I pushed her away. If only I could turn back the clock and change my answer.

"Do you remember when you gave me my nickname *Pink*?" she asked wistfully.

"I do." I picked up her free hand and entwined our fingers. "You were at Mount Laurel for a Christmas party wearing a pink dress with white fur on the edges. I couldn't resist the play on words because, well...immature college student mind at work and all." I pointed a thumb at my chest. "I said, 'You really are the cutest little pink elf in all of elfdom, so I'ma hafta call you Pink from now on.' You were not bothered by my teasing even a tiny bit because you turned the tables on me and said, 'I am Pink and you are Gray. The colors were already in our names, you big dummy.'"

She cracked a smile that lasted for too short a time before it went away. "I still have that dress somewhere, because I can't bear to get rid of it."

"Why do you keep it?" I asked, interested in her answer.

"Because it reminds me of a time when—when I-I didn't know what hurt felt l-l-like..." she trailed off on a sad sob.

"I would take that hurt away from you if I could. He did you wrong and you have every right to feel sad, Reese. I just wish I'd given you a different answer before you ever met him, so you never would've had to go through any of this at all."

"But where would that leave me now, Gray?" She took her hand away from mine and brushed the tear off her cheek with her finger.

"You'd be with me, and you wouldn't be hurting or sad right now. I'd make sure of it. All you have to do is say *yes* to my question."

Reese lifted her eyes up to mine again, but this time her expression looked a lot less vulnerable. The Steel Magnolia thing? She had that look in her eyes. "No, I would need more than that."

"What more do you need? Tell me and I'll do my best to give it to you."

"I don't think you can, based on what you said two years ago." She picked up her wine again and drank probably half of the glass before putting it down with a small shake of her head. "So, what has changed so much for you since then? Will you tell me where this marriage idea is really coming from?"

This was where my plan started to veer off the rails really fuckin' quick. I wanted to be able to tell her I was in love with her, but every time I got to the verge of saying it, I dialed back. I didn't want to be callus and say I loved her because there was a billion-dollar fortune at stake. I don't think Reese wanted to hear that was my reason, any more than I wanted to admit it. "Our timing has not been good, I know—"

She cut my lame-ass excuse off like a sharp knife slicing through a tomato. "Tim said he loved me long before he asked me to marry him. You did just the opposite of that, Grayson." Whenever Reese brought out my full name she had my full attention. It meant whatever she had to say was important and I should listen. It was weird we had such an understanding at this deep of a level, but we did. Pink and Gray did indeed know each other very well, and there was a whole lot of respect embedded in that knowledge.

"How so?" I asked.

"Well, two years ago you told me you couldn't love anyone, because the emotion just wasn't in your heart, and now you've just asked me to marry you—*again.*"

"But that was before—"

She held up her palm to shut me down. "Tim couldn't follow through on the marriage, and you cannot deliver on the love. I know you care about me, Gray, I do know, but I need more than just your affection and the approval of our families. Neither of my proposals of marriage, from Tim or from you, are what I would ever choose now. I want— and deserve—to have it all."

"Yes, I agree. You do deserve to have it all, and I believe I can give it to you."

"Oh, is that right?" she countered. "And just how are you going to give me the love you don't feel?"

"By taking you upstairs to my room in this hotel, named after President Thomas

Jefferson, and making love to you until you can't remember your own name, the name of any president who has ever served this fine nation, let alone that idiot who broke your heart two months ago. Reese, if you just let me love you, then I know I *will* feel it."

"So, let me get this right. You're saying if I go upstairs with you, and we spend the night in your bed doing all of those things that lovers do together when they are naked and in bed, you believe you will feel differently about me than you have in the past?"

"Definitely." My brain (cock) heard the words "naked" and "bed" in the same sentence sail off her tongue and stopped listening at that point.

"And this magical transformation will happen exactly when, Gray?"

"When I'm buried inside you and can see into your pretty green-gold eyes as you're coming all over my cock." *Shit. I just said that out loud I think.*

"Yes, you did," she answered as she stood up from the table. "Get us another bottle of wine, please."

I stared up at her with an equal measure of confusion and fear. She was either saying yes to the sex, or planning my death with a broken bottle to the throat. Maybe both.

Wasn't sure.

Didn't care.

Reese found my indecision comical, because she had to bite down on her bottom lip to suppress the laughter I could clearly see behind her eyes.

"I'm ready whenever you are, so hurry up."

I FOLLOWED HER OUT OF THE RESTAURANT LIKE a starved dog after a platter of steaks. I'm sure anyone who saw me with her would've confirmed this, but thankfully it was a hot August night in DC, and The Jefferson just happened to be very quiet. We saw no one. This could have been because I was incapable of seeing anyone else in the room once Reese agreed to my *suggestion* we go on upstairs to my suite and work this controversy out while naked and horizontal in my bed. *Although, naked and vertical would also work for me just fine.*

When we stepped inside the elevator, I wasted no time backing her into the corner, the freedom to press myself against her and experience what her body felt like beneath mine, no longer a fantasy.

She was soft.

I was so fucking hard.

She smelled so good.

I was intoxicated by her scent.

"I do wish you would kiss me," she said, her eyes focusing on my lips.

Some faint sliver of caution had hung on in my conscious mind to wait until we were behind the closed door of my suite—which was a very good thing. Because in walked the Secretary of State and the Speaker of the House to ride in the elevator with us up to the top.

Now, I don't claim to be an expert on sociology by any means, but I had enough brain matter firing up in my dome to understand the image of the State Attorney General, grandson of President Grayson T. Lash, dry-humping the great-great-granddaughter of President Theodore Pinkarver, in the elevator at The Jefferson, would not ride silently into the sunset.

"Ahh, I thought that was you, Mr. Lash," Secretary Carlin said.

"Madam Secretary, Madam Speaker, hello. How are you ladies this evening?" I offered my hand to each of them in turn; praying to God my jacket covered the indecent display putting on a show behind my fly. *Fuck me.*

"Is that little Reese Pinkarver all grown up, you are guarding in the corner, Mr. Lash?" Speaker Morris asked while eyeing the wine bottle in my other hand.

Reese giggled from behind me and gave a friendly wave. "Yes, it's me, Madam Speaker. Gray has taken me to dinner, and now he's invited me up to his suite so we can have some really good se—"

"Some—good talk—ahh...Reese and I are *talking* about our plans for the immediate future."

I'd stopped Reese from sharing the real plans for our immediate future—defiling each other in my bed over the next three hours or so—but I only stopped her from sharing those plans out loud. Anybody could connect the dots.

*Oh, that sounded bad.*

Worse than bad was a lot more accurate of just how I had sounded in my pathetic attempt to converse politely with Speaker Olivia Morris.

So, I topped off my "worse than bad" with a little shot of "stupid fucking moron" by asking, "What are you ladies up to tonight?"

Audra Carlin, Secretary of State of the United States of America, shot me a quick wink. "Nothing we can discuss, Mr. Lash, but I assure you it's not as interesting as whatever you have planned with Ms. Pinkarver this evening."

# CHAPTER 7

## GRAY

Reese was still giggling as we burst out of the stairwell that opened up into the hallway leading to my suite. Our encounter with two of the nation's highest ranking public servants inspired us to get off the elevator and take the stairs the rest of the way.

It crossed my mind that she'd had a little too much to drink for what we were about to do, but the part of me that wanted her so badly just couldn't stop from taking what she was offering. There was no more ability for rational thinking on my part. Nothing left in me to steer us in another direction.

The sound of the door shutting behind us worked like a signal for me. I was on her the second the wine was abandoned on an entryway table. With two free hands I could touch and feel her properly—and keep my promise to make her forget her name.

She lifted her lips, offering them so sweetly it made me pause for a second, because I knew once I gave in, it would be the end of my restraint. I'd do every dirty thing she'd let me do to her, while honoring any special requests, of course.

I had been trained to remember a gentleman listens to a lady.

I took her face in my hands and backed her up. Her lips parted and her eyes opened wide as I flattened her against the wall and kissed her for the first time. A real kiss with my lips pressed against hers, intimate and deep. I pushed my tongue inside for a taste. When she responded by meeting me stroke for stroke, the sexual tension increased tenfold. I felt her hands touching me, her palm pressing against my hard cock through clothing I wished would die in a fire. If she kept stroking me, a fire was probably a real possibility. I needed to take in more of her but couldn't stop with what my mouth was doing.

I moved my hands down her body simultaneously, our mouths never separating as I found new parts of her to explore. Her slender neck, the curves of her magnificent tits, and finally, all the way down to her equally magnificent ass. My hands stopped there, and I used my grip on her ass to pull her off her feet and up against my body. I felt her legs wrap around me securely, and also the throbbing of my cock from having her so close to me. Desperately linked in a frenzy of kissing, it went on and on, our bodies moving against each other. Connected by heat and seeking friction, the barriers of clothing were our only enemy.

Shoes dropped from her feet with clunking sounds as they met the floor.

I started walking at some point, carrying her wrapped around me with her legs split wide—right at the spot where my cock was agonizingly waiting for an introduction inside.

Somehow I got us to the bed.

By sheer force of will, I separated my mouth from hers, and dropped her down onto the bed. She fell back onto the mattress with a soft bounce and stared up at me. Her eyes were wild as she caught sight of the tenting from my cock. The admiration in her eyes as she swept them back up to focus on my face was pretty fucking clear. And so goddamn sexy I had to suppress the urge to whip out my cock and come all over her pretty pink lips.

We stared at each other as I toed off my shoes and shrugged out of my jacket, letting it drop to the floor with a soft thud.

Reese sat up on her knees in the bed and reached down to find the bottom edge of her dress. I held my breath as she pulled it up her body and then over her head, sending it down to land on top of my jacket. This left her only in some really sexy lingerie that needed to be peeled off her body.

With my teeth.

The black lace served as a mere enhancement to what she'd been born with: long legs I wanted wrapped around me again, a delectable ass I wanted in my lap, and perfectly round tits I wanted overflowing in my hands once I took the bra off her.

She lifted her arms, beckoning me toward the edge of the bed. Her small, delicate fingers started in on my tie, and then my shirt. I stood frozen in time and space, while her hands were busy with my clothes. Once my shirt and tie had met the floor, she efficiently removed my belt, then my pants. I was right in step with her, working in tandem to get us closer to that place we both wanted to be.

Naked. So very naked.

"Take off the rest," I said, while peeling off my socks.

It was her turn now.

And she did not disappoint, because her hands went behind her back and released the tiny hooks of her bra at lightning speed, the tight hold of the lace cups coming loose as the two halves separated.

I held my breath as she brought her arms through the straps...and then the bra was gone.

Just Reese, remained.

And also a pair of lacy black panties that

were dangerously close to a violent death.

Restraint was all but gone, once I could see her beautiful, beautiful breasts with my eyes.

God in heaven, help me.

"You are so perfectly stunning," I said, closing the distance between us.

My mouth went to her neck first and then trailed down to the curve at the top of her right breast, all while kissing my way to the tightened bud at the center. My mouth found her nipple and sucked around the peak, drawing back on it until it popped out from between my lips. She protested the loss of my mouth on her with a sexy moan that only served to spur me on.

I went in again and again, alternating between the two with sucking pulls, until she was an arching, writhing creature ready to be fucked. It sounded so much dirtier in my mind than it was. Because *this* act was a thing of beauty between us. Reese was beautiful, and we were beautiful together.

Feeling her grinding against my thigh in desperation sent me into overdrive. I pulled back and stripped out of my shorts, freeing the beast before he turned violent on me. I did the same thing to her black lace panties as I had with my shorts—flung them somewhere across the room.

"I want in you, Reese."

"I want it too. Gray, please—please I need to feel you."

"I'm clean, but do you want me using a condom?" I managed to ask at the last second.

"No—Depo shot—it's okay if you don't. I trust you," she breathed up at me, her hand smoothing down my stomach and abdomen to find my cock and wrap around it in a tight grip.

I hissed out a groan of pleasure as she gave it a stroke. Her touch...It was like nothing else I'd ever felt before. I'd noticed earlier when she touched me through two layers of clothing, the electricity fired off shocks throughout my whole body.

I slipped my hands to the back of her thighs and spread her wide open. The sight of her wet slit waiting for my cock was all I needed. My tongue and her pussy would get to know each other a little later on. Right now my cock wanted in, and he wasn't waiting for a second request. Just the first one from her was plenty.

I nudged the tip between her folds and pushed in just enough to test her readiness. Slippery wet heat burned through the sensitive flesh, and we both gasped at the contact. Reese lifted her hips to try to take in more of my cock, and that was the tipping point for me.

I was done with limits.

I thrust forward all the way to my balls,

fitting like a glove inside her. She cried my name as she took in every inch of me, gripping my shaft with a heat so intense, I was sure we'd both incinerate. My mouth came down over hers with a deep plunge of my tongue, swallowing her soft cries and moans greedily. I wanted—I needed her mouth and her pussy together at the same time. As I started to move in and out of her in a building rhythm, I realized I needed every part of Reese she was willing to give me. I just needed her.

We were going to fuck until we both came.

And then we'd switch it up and fuck in a different position until we both came some more.

We would fuck and come as many times as we wanted, until we needed sleep more than we needed to fuck. It would happen eventually, and when it did, she would be in my bed sleeping next to me for the rest of the night.

Then in the morning, I would ask her to marry me, again.

And this time she would say *yes*.

# CHAPTER 8

## REESE

My head hurt so badly; I was surely in aneurysm territory with the pounding. But no, the real reason for the headache was too many glasses of wine the night before, combined with *who* was naked and snoring softly beside me in the bed. Gray was a beautiful man in all of his glory, just as God had made him. I could watch him sleeping for a long time and be fully entertained. The rise and fall of his sculpted chest, the shock of sandy hair across his forehead, the calmness showing in his features while at rest. In fact, he looked so very peaceful, I made the decision not to wake him.

It would be best this way.

Easier on him, and better for me.

I had no business sleeping with Grayson Lash, and pretending this could become something real and permanent. My heart was still broken by Tim, unready for more torture. And it would end up being torture for Gray, if he persisted in this marriage thing with me.

Unfortunately, I couldn't remember any specific details about the sex from last night, but it was clear we'd done it. There had been a lot of sex, from what I could figure when I went into the bathroom to put myself back together. I might not remember all the erotic details, but I did recall the conversation Gray and I had at dinner about love and marriage. He didn't believe in love for himself, but was willing to give his theory a shot with me. That being, if he made love to me, he might feel differently about me afterward. I didn't buy into his theoretical argument, but I didn't blame him for trying either. Gray wasn't using me. If anything, I was using him. He was simply hoping to make the best of a situation into which we'd both been born. I understood Grayson Lash better than most people probably ever would. I had the very same baggage to carry around on my shoulders, forever. But the fact remained, he didn't love me, and I was too raw from Tim to open myself up to more heartbreak. And I was certain Gray could break my heart, if I gave him half a chance.

I looked like Sleeping Beauty in a reverse negative when I let myself out of his hotel suite. I had my walk-of-shame through the lobby of The Jefferson, before making my way into the waiting Uber I'd requested from my phone.

Gray would find my note on the elegant stationery supplied by the hotel when he woke up. He'd be angry at first, but eventually he would understand where I was coming from. In time, we'd go back to our normal relationship, and last night would feel far less important than it probably felt right now.

*Dear Grayson,*

*I don't want to discuss what happened last night between us. Please respect this request from me, as your dear friend you would not want to hurt, any more than I would ever want to hurt you. I am not able to do this with you right now, so I ask you to please understand where I am coming from in a broken relationship.*

*My heart simply requires more time to heal*

*before I try to open it up to another person.*

*I know the content of your character is excellent, just as I know you are a fine man, who will do so much good for others in your role as a public servant, however highly you aspire to serve.*

*Please take care.*

*With love,*

*Reese*

*Present day...*

HORATIO MATCHED GRAY'S SUIT PERFECTLY. The exact same monochromatic festival of gray-ness blended together so well it looked intentional. My usually very protective kitty planted himself on Gray's lap, and proceeded to purr himself into an enchantment broken only by the occasional twitching of his tail. *Traitor.*

Once we were inside my apartment, I told Gray to have a seat, and wait for me while I changed into something that wasn't a wedding gown.

As I roughly removed the silk and tulle creation, and kicked it into a corner of my bedroom, I realized Gray had followed my directions without a word of challenge. For once. The mood between us was tense, and we were both exhausted, but I'd let him know earlier that he and I were having this conversation tonight. He wasn't excused until I said so.

Maybe he was indulging me because he'd been so traumatized by my asthma attack/ambulance/hospital ordeal. Even though I was fine, and had responded to my rescue inhaler exactly as I was supposed to, Gray was not yet convinced. His experience tonight with me at the ER had really scared him.

When I emerged from my bedroom wearing yoga pants and my favorite pink sweater, Gray and Horatio's bromance was in full swing. This from the cat who hissed at everyone, except for my grandmother. I wouldn't care to lay odds on my cat being a beneficiary in my grandmother's will, either.

I sat down opposite of them in my big fluffy chair, actually feeling comfortable for the first time in many hours.

"Don't the two of you look cozy," I offered as a greeting to break the ice. Everything felt awkward now, but I was determined to forge ahead and get my answers to some questions that had been bothering me for a while now.

Gray's eyes flicked over me quickly and then refocused on Horatio. "He's awesome," he said, while repeatedly stroking down Horatio's back from head to tail. "He would love it at Mount Laurel."

"My grandmother got Horatio for me two years ago as a birthday present."

"I remember you telling me he and Dr. Voldemort did not get along," Gray said, while keeping his eyes focused on Horatio. "Smart cat."

"I don't think I have ever heard you refer to him by name, Gray."

Silence infused with strains of purring cat was all I got by way of a response.

"Tim. His name is Dr. Timothy Pellton—"

"I know the cocksucker's name—I just don't want to speak it."

I sighed. "Why do you hate him so much?"

"Why don't you hate him enough?" he asked angrily.

"Are you afraid I would take him back? Is that why?" God, I would *never* take Tim back after what he did to me.

Again, with more of the silent treatment combined with ultra-focused cat petting.

"Gray?"

"Hmm?"

He finally looked up to meet me eye to eye. Gray was teetering on the edge of losing his self-control, and I sensed it wouldn't take much to push him over.

I decided to give him a shove anyway.

"You'd better start talking, Grayson Lash, or you can get the hell out of my house."

"Okay, you want honesty, you got it, baby," he snapped. "Where do I fuckin' start?"

"How about start with why you hate Tim so much?"

"He got you to fall in love with him and then agree to marry him."

"Why do you care who I love or who I

marry? It's all so very stupid. You never wanted me until I was with him. That's the honest-to-God-truth, Gray, and you know it. Please tell me why you want to marry me now and not before."

"I have always cared about you. Pink. Always."

"That is not what I am asking you. I know you care about me. Can't you just be honest with me for two damn minutes?"

"You were always supposed to marry me," he shouted back.

Horatio howled and took off like a streak of gray smoke, disappearing from Gray's lap in a nanosecond. Most likely he was now hiding under my bed, and would stay there until he felt good and ready to come out. Horatio did what *he* wanted, when *he* wanted.

"But you never cared who I dated. You told me we could never be together right after your father died. You did not want *me*, Gray.

It was not the other way around."

"Well, I changed my mind, okay? I do want you. I want you to marry me, and be my wife, and live with me, and together we will make a wonderful life."

"I've heard that part loud and clear, Grayson. What you won't tell me is the reason *why*."

"Well, I'd like to know why you keep running away from me. Why you left me with no explanation beyond a fuckin' Dear John on hotel letterhead, after the night we shared two months ago. It must not have meant much to you. It did to me, though. That night we had together was something so right—"

"But I explained in my letter that I need some time. Why can't you accept that I need time to put Tim behind me?"

"Because *we don't have* any more motherfuckin' time to spare!"

"What does that even mean?" I snarled.

"It means the difference of a billion-dollar fortune going to our son—or not."

"I knew it. This has been about money from the very beginning. How disgusting." I pretended outrage, but it was nothing I hadn't already suspected. Gray was simply putting legs to the idea.

"Do you even grasp the concept of a billion-dollar legacy, Reese? Talk to your grandfather if you don't believe me. I went to Harvard with his contracts lawyer. James Blakney in Boston can give you every detail. Theodore set this plan in motion with my father fifteen years ago. We get married *before* you turn twenty-five. And then we make some sons whose surname will legally change to Pinkarver-Lash. How can you even act surprised by this news?"

I felt my heart drop to the floor. My grandfather was going to try to control my life from beyond the grave. To manipulate me by influencing the destiny of my innocent children who hadn't even been born yet.

"This is our game plan, devised by others long ago." He gestured with his hand back and forth between us. "We are merely the players in the game. Did no one ever mention the rules to you, princess?" he asked bitterly.

*No, they did not.*

"But what about love?" The tears were coming so hard now I could barely see his face anymore.

"Love has no place in politics, or games of chess. You play, and do your best to win. That's how it works. Love tears people apart, and then it destroys them."

"I don't believe that at all."

"You should. Take a long hard look at yourself, Reese. You're terrified to move on from the *love* you feel for a piece of shit who discarded you for the right price. He did that for money. What did you just call it?

Disgusting, wasn't it?"

"No, he did not..." I sobbed.

"Yes, he did, Reese. Pellton did not deserve you, any more than he could have made you a happy life."

I didn't want to believe Tim could have betrayed me so carelessly, but deep down I knew Gray was speaking the truth. Gray had always been truthful with me, and trustworthy, and respectful, and loyal.

The weight of fear can be devastating, and so I needed to face my fears once and for all, to conquer their hold on me.

"Please leave my house," I said numbly, "I want to be alone now."

AFTER HE'D GONE, I CRAWLED INTO MY BED

with Horatio and cried myself to sleep. My tears couldn't wash away the terrible look of defeat on Gray's face, though. It was burned into my mind. We'd exchanged some harsh words last night. Some of them, I would painfully remember. Some, I would choose to forget. The truth did hurt, but at least it was an honest hurt. For myself, I would rather be hurt by truth, than by a lie.

When I separated out the facts, I could see exactly how Tim had hurt me with lies, and conversely, Gray with the truth. This revelation changed nothing to stem the pain, though.

Gray was correct about love tearing people apart.

Gray was so right about many things I wasn't yet ready to own. The hardest part was when he'd asked me if *I* was in love with him. My answering silence had been deafening.

He told me I knew where to find him if I ever had a change of heart, right before he walked out. Meaning he hadn't written me off completely. He'd *still* be there for me if I ever needed him.

And that was the caliber of man that made up Grayson T. Lash III. Solid, dependable, loyal and truthful. A laundry list of admirable qualities, attached to a man who was so much more than I ever hoped to find, in someone *I loved.*

A PHONE CALL THE NEXT MORNING WOKE ME from a dead sleep. I let it go to voicemail, until I heard the caller identify himself. I fumbled to get it before he hung up, and for once, achieved success. "Dr. Romero, hello."

"Good morning, Reese. I'm so glad you

picked up, because I don't leave messages for this sort of thing."

"What is it? I feel completely fine after a night of sleep." Not really, but definitely the more socially appropriate response.

"Ah, good. Glad to hear it. This is about your blood test results that came in a few hours after you'd left us last night, that require me to notify the patient personally as soon as possible."

"Oh?"

"Yes, your HCG levels indicate that you are pregnant now."

# CHAPTER 9

## REESE

My mother might have been young when she had me, but she learned very quickly how to protect and insulate me away from the powerful influences of my father's family. By the time they were back in our lives, she was legally and emotionally in control of the relationship. After all, my mother held all the cards once my father was gone, and there was not a thing Theodore Pinkarver could do to change it.

At least not until I legally became an adult.

When I turned eighteen, there was some talk of a new will in place that would name me as a major beneficiary, but I didn't know very much more than that. I'd never really been interested in how much my grandparents were worth. I knew they were wealthy, but only in the sense that a child looks up to the adults who oversee the purse strings. It made logical sense that families of former presidents weren't ever going to be on welfare, or food stamps, or homeless.

My first action after hanging up with Dr. Romero was to count back to my last Depo shot and do the math. No method of birth control was one hundred percent fail proof, but I had to concede that I'd been late for my shot by a good month. The safe zone is one shot every three months, so it was possible a few of the little swimmers were not deterred during my night with Gray seven weeks ago. More sex increases the chances. We had provided several opportunities in a single night from what I could figure out. All things considered, I had been under the influence, and yet what little I did remember of the experience, had been Gray asking if I wanted him to use a condom.

I'd very easily (stupidly) told him no.

This was not Gray's fault.

It was mine.

And it was well past time for me to speak with my mother.

"Reese, my sweet baby girl, why are you crying?"

"Mama, I have messed things up, and I'm

so scared. I'm afraid for what will happen to us now."

"Us?"

"I'm pregnant with Gray's child and I've hurt him badly—and I just found out about the money—and I've been to the ER with asthma, and found out that Tim left me, because Grandfather paid him off..." I'm sure there was a great deal more incoherent babbling inserted in between my crying meltdown that went into our conversation, but I didn't care, once I heard my mother's voice on the other end of the line telling me she was on her way to me.

It would take an entire day for her to get to DC, though.

She gave me some very good advice to consider during the time it would take her to travel to me. I listened to my mother, because she knew a thing or two about being single and pregnant with an American presidential legacy, now didn't she?

"I know you are terrified and emotional, sweetheart, but now you have to consider the welfare of your child over what you might want for yourself. From now on, whatever's best for your baby, is what is best for you as well."

"You're right, Mama, of course, but the things I said to Gray were cruel—"

"Gray is a grown man, and he will get over it—as will you. If there is one thing I am sure of, Reese darling, is that Gray loves you and he has for years. He just doesn't know exactly how to say the words, but I think that's about to change."

"No, he told me he'd never been in love, and it was a waste of emotion that destroyed lives."

"Oh really, well, I am quite certain that our dear Mr. Lash is about to be served an entire meal of crow on that particular matter, which he will happily eat down to the very last morsel."

"No, Mama, I don't think so," I said sadly.

"I want you to think about what you would want if this situation were reversed. Would you want to be told about the baby?"

"Yes, of course."

"Don't you think Gray should hear the news from you first?"

"Yes," I admitted weakly.

"Don't sign any contracts until I'm there and we have lawyers present, but you can at least tell the father of your child he has a baby on the way."

MY HEART POUNDED IN MY CHEST SO HARD I could feel my whole body vibrate with every thudding beat. I could see my fingers shaking as I tapped out a text to Gray on my phone.

**Reese:** I need to see you in person. I have something very important to tell you. Are you still in town?

**Gray:** I stayed over at Lance's place last night. I have something important to say, too. Where are you now?

**Reese:** On the metro. I am coming to you.

**Gray:** CAPITOL SOUTH Station?

**Reese:** Yes.

# CHAPTER 10

## GRAY

*I am coming to you.*

Reese was coming to me. The ache I'd felt since she'd asked me to leave her place last night lifted immediately, as if the elephant who'd been sitting on my chest had just up and moved his fat ass to sit somewhere else. Thank God.

I bolted out of Oakley's front door and

headed up New Jersey Avenue to the metro station where I would meet my woman. My lovely Pink was coming to me, and I would be there waiting for her when she arrived. I knew exactly what to say to her this time. I had all the words that needed to be said, ready on the tip of my tongue. What had seemed so terrifying to me just a day ago, did not scare me anymore.

Not waking up to her beside me every morning, scared me. Never introducing her as my wife, scared me. Never being inside her again when she was coming, scared me. I had a lot of fuckin' fears where my Pink was concerned, but not one of those fears hinged upon saying three very important words, I would happily shout down to her from the rooftop of the Library of Congress at CAPITOL SOUTH station for all to hear. Hopefully, that shit would be Facebook Live'd by someone, and on the seven o'clock news.

I ran as fast as my legs would take me.

We saw each other at the same time. She was walking fast when she spotted me. Her steps slowed, but she kept closing the distance between us. Closer to where I stood waiting. Reese had said she would come to me, and so that was what we were doing here.

Keeping our promise.

I could see she'd been crying. I wanted to kiss and lick away every trace of her tears, and I would later—after we got this important business out of the way.

She brought a hand to her heart and held it there as she took more steps toward me, her long blond hair blowing back gently in the autumn breeze. I noticed she had on the pink sweater she'd worn last night. The pale color had always suited her.

My Pink looked lovely in pink.

I held out my arms, because I just

couldn't wait another second before holding her against me.

She understood and accepted my gesture by running the last bit of the way. And then she was in my arms, and I was spinning her in a circle. I kissed her as if my life depended upon her lips to survive the next minutes. I'm sure my life did require her kisses for survival, but eventually she pulled back to meet me eye to eye.

"Gray, I have to tell you something," she said with her palm to the side of my cheek. "It's very important."

"Please let me say mine first. It's very important too."

She nodded and looked up, giving me her full attention. I held up three fingers and said, "Three words. I love you."

"You do?"

"Yes, I love you. I learned that loving you

is not a thing I can choose to do, or not do. Love is something I finally understand after all these years. And I only *understand it* in the context of you. I love you, Reese Amelia Pinkarver, and to prove it, I won't ask you to marry me again."

"You *won't* marry me?"

"That's not exactly what I said. There is more to add to the sentence. I won't *ask* you to marry me again, at any time before your birthday comes. So, you go on ahead and turn twenty-five, baby. I can wait for you as long as you need me to wait. I also don't need your grandfather's billion-dollar legacy. Let him donate it to some worthy charity in your father's name, if that suits him better. I have enough money already, and in case you did not hear me say it before, I love you, so the only thing I cannot do without, is *you*."

Her smile lit up her beautiful face so brightly it glowed. "Gray, I have three words for you, too."

I figured she might throw me an *I love you* if I was very, very lucky. So, when she gave me her three words, my knees buckled, and I nearly went down.

"We are pregnant."

"We are?"

But she wasn't finished.

"I have a couple more three-worders for you, Grayson T. Lash III. 'I love you' and 'Let's get married' tie everything up for us all nice and neat, don't you agree, my love?"

Nodding enthusiastically, I went back to kissing my lovely Pink in front of the Library of Congress and the CAPITOL SOUTH metro station. I figured I had to be the luckiest man in all of America right about now, so the best plan for me was just to appreciate my good fortune, and my girl.

I could hear cheers and congratulations

all around us, the gathering crowd clearly enjoying our show. Thanks to my buddy, Lance, who was putting it out on Facebook Live for us, we'd be able to watch it tonight on the seven o'clock news with the rest of the world.

Or any other time I needed a reminder of what real love looks like.

THE END

*-for now-*

# A Request

If you enjoyed *Lovely Pink*, please consider leaving a review.

I thank you for reading my book!

For my newsletter and information on upcoming books and events, sign up on my website below. You will receive a welcome message and a FREE book just for signing up. *I will not spam your inbox.*

I send a monthly email with news about my books, special deals, and always a freebie for you in every newsletter.

Only GREAT stuff.

*Sign up at:*

www.rainemiller.com

# A Note from Raine

*Lovely Pink*, this wonderful little story I absolutely adored writing, has a crossover book in HUSBAND MATERIAL, with both stories part of a new world for the direction of my creative plotting. There are good things happening down in the Carolinas for some new characters you'll meet in future books.

Readers already familiar with my work are used to the little connections I like to sprinkle in my books as Easter Eggs for them to find. For the new reader these Easter Eggs will not stand out in any remarkable way, but if you know my other books, including the historicals, then you will find those little gems placed here and there in the words and will know them when they appear.

Grayson Lash and Reese Pinkarver originally from *Capitol South*, the novella I put in the *Love In Transit* anthology a few years ago—have a connection to Gage Danielson, the hero of HUSBAND MATERIAL. Reese is a cousin to Gage...who is also a very close friend of Grayson Lash...who even makes a small appearance in HUSBAND MATERIAL. You might have noticed that Gray mentions a law school buddy in Boston who is head counsel for Reese's grandparents and the future probate of their will. One James R. Blakney. *winky wink* These books are ALL connected in little ways.

And lastly, I'd be remiss if I didn't make a comment about a certain character who hosted the Halloween party where Reese and Gray start their evening in this book. A character who appears in my Blackstone

Affair series as a villain of sorts—Lance Oakley—but who also has a very surprising backstory that I hope to tell one day. I know some readers may not be ready to hear Lance's story just yet, but it's percolating in my head and I know I'd love to tell it in the future. There is so much more to Lance than what has been told in the books thus far. For now, just know that he's living in Washington DC practicing law and good friends with both Gray and Reese.

And just so you know...Reese has a LOT of cousins out there, so more connections are coming in future books down the road. This is what I do for fun.

Exciting times ahead.

*xo Raine*

# ABOUT THE AUTHOR

RAINE MILLER is a *New York Times*, *USA Today*, and *Wall Street Journal* bestselling author since 2012. Before that, she spent two decades teaching kiddos to read–something she's most proud of. These days, writing steamy romance stories pretty much fills up the hours... for which she keeps pinching herself to make sure she's not dreaming.

#Truth

She has a handsome husband, two amazing sons, and two very bouncy Italian greyhounds to keep her busy the rest of the time. Her boys know she writes romance books but gratefully have zero interest in reading even a single one. Thank God!

When she's not writing she's likely deep into a hockey game cheering on her beloved *VEGAS GOLDEN KNIGHTS* and dreaming up a new book. The greyhounds are likely to be in her lap while she writes the books or watches hockey—both dogs at the same time.

She loves to hear from readers and chat about the characters she's created.

You can connect with Raine on Facebook in her group, **Raine Miller Romance Readers**. She pops in to visit most days because it's a super happy place where romance awesomeness abounds day in and day out with the most amazing readers on earth. "My readers are the heart and soul of what keeps me writing the words."

#AlsoTruth

# BOOKS BY RAINE MILLER

## THE ROTHVALE LEGACY
PRICELESS, Part 1
MY LORD, Part 2

## BLACKSTONE DYNASTY
FILTHY RICH
FILTHY LIES

## THE BLACKSTONE AFFAIR
NAKED, Part 1
ALL IN, Part 2
EYES WIDE OPEN, Part 3
RARE and PRECIOUS THINGS, Part 4

## CONTEMPORARY ROMANCE
CHERRY GIRL
HUSBAND MATERIAL
LOVELY PINK

# HOCKEY ROMANCE
### WRITING as *Brit DeMille*

CRUSHED, *Vegas Crush #1*
SIN SHOT, *Vegas Crush #2*
RED ROCKET, *Vegas Crush #3*
PUCK MONEY, *Vegas Crush #4*
SMOKESHOW, *Vegas Crush #5*
The KEEPER, *Vegas Crush #6*

# HISTORICAL ROMANCE

The PASSION of DARIUS
The UNDOING of a LIBERTINE

*Historical Prequels to The Rothvale Legacy*
The MUSE
The ROGUE *(soon)*

# WEDDING NIGHT DIARIES
### LORD BLACKWOOD'S VIRGIN

*Lovely Pink*

# Notes

# Notes

www.ingramcontent.com/pod-product-compliance
Lightning Source LLC
Chambersburg PA
CBHW070458170726
48291CB00008B/2560